THE MANIC
CLOWN

THE MANIC CLOWN

ALDIVAN TORRES

Canary Of Joy

Contents

1 1

I

The Manic Clown
Aldivan Torres
The Manic Clown

Author: Aldivan Torres
2020- Aldivan Torres
All rights reserved
Series: The Perverted Sisters

This book, including all its parts, is copyrighted and cannot be reproduced without the permission of the author, resold or transferred.

Aldivan Torres, born in Brazil, is a literary artist. Promises with his writings to delight the public and lead him to the delights of pleasure. After all, sex is one of the best things there is.

The manic clown

Sunday came and with him a lot of news in town. Among them, the arrival of a circus named "Superstar", famous all over Brazil. That's all we talked about in the area. Curious innately, the two sisters programmed to attend the opening of the show scheduled for this very night.

Near the schedule, the two of them were already ready to go out after a special dinner for their bachelorette celebration. Dressed for the gala, both paraded in simultaneous, where they left the house and entered the garage. Entering the car, they start with one of them coming down and closing the garage. With the return of the same, the journey can be resumed without any further problems.

Leaving district Saint Christopher, head towards district Boa Vista at the other end of the city, the capital of the hinterland with around eighty thousand inhabitants. As they walk along the quiet avenues, they are amazed by the architecture, the Christmas decoration, the spirits of the people, the churches, the mountains they seemed to speak of, the fragrant puns exchanged in complicity, the sound of loud rock, the French perfume, the conversations about politics, business, society, parties, northeastern culture and secrets. Anyway, they were totally relaxed, anxious, nervous as well as concentrated.

On the way, instantly, a fine rain fall. Against expectations, girls open the vehicle windows making small drops of water lubricate their faces. This gesture shows their simplicity and authenticity, true self-astral champions. This is the best option for people. What's the point of removing failures, the restlessness and pain of the past? They wouldn't take them anywhere. That's why they were happy through their choices. Though the world judged them, they didn't care because they owned their destiny. Happy birthday to them!

About ten minutes out, they're already in the parking lot attached to the circus. They close the car, walk a few meters into the inner courtyard of the environment. For coming early, they sit on the first bleachers. While you're waiting for the show, they buy popcorn, beer, drop the bullshit and silent puns. There was nothing better than being in the circus!

Forty minutes later, the show is initiated. Among the attractions are joking clowns, acrobats, trapeze artists, contortionists, death globe, magicians, jugglers and a musical show. For three hours, they live magical moments, funny, distracted, play, fall in love, at last, live. With the breakup of the show, they make sure to go to the dressing room and greet one of the clowns. He had accomplished the stunt of cheering them up like it never happened.

Up on stage, you have to get a line. Coincidentally, they're the last ones to go into the dressing room. There, they find a totally disfigured clown, away from the stage.

"We came here to congratulate you on your great show. There's a God's gift in it! He watched Belinha.

"Your words and your gestures have shaken my

spirit. I don't know, but I noticed a sadness in your eyes. Am I right?

"Thank you both for the words. What are your names? Answered the clown.

"My name is Amelinha!

"My name is Belinha.

"Nice to meet you. You can call me Gilberto! I've actually been through enough pain in this life. One of them was the recent separation from my wife. You must understand it's not easy to separate from your wife after 20 years of living, right? Regardless, I am pleased to fulfill my art.

"Poor guy! I'm sorry! (Amelinha).

"What can we do to cheer him up? (Belinha).

"I don't know how. After my wife's breakup, I miss her so much. (Gilberto).

"We can fix this, can't we, sister? (Belinha).

"Sure. You're a good-looking man. (Amelinha)

"Thank you, girls. You guys are wonderful. Exclaimed Gilberto.

Without waiting any longer, the white, tall, strong, dark-eyed manly went undressing, and the ladies followed his example. Totally naked, the trio went into the foreplay right there on the floor. More than an exchange of emotions and swearing, sex amused them and cheered them up. In those brief moments, they felt parts of a greater force, the love of God. Through love, they reached the greater ecstasy a human could achieve.

Finishing the act, they dress up and say goodbye. That one more step and the conclusion that came was that man was a wild wolf. A manic clown you'll never forget. No more, they leave the circus moving to the parking lot. They're getting in the car starting their way back. The next few days were promised more surprises.

The second dawn has come more beautiful than ever. Early in the morning, our friends are pleased to feel the heat of the sun and the breeze wandering in their faces. These contrasts caused in the physical aspect of the same a good feeling of freedom, contentment, satisfaction, and joy. They were ready, for, to face a new day.

However, they concentrate their forces culminating on their lifting. The next step is to go to the suite and do it with extreme vagrancy as if they were of the state of Bahia. Not to hurt our dear neighbors, of course. The land of all saints is a spectacular place full of culture, history and secular traditions. Long live Bahia.

In the bathroom, they take off their clothes by the strange feeling they weren't alone. Who's ever heard of the legend of the blonde bathroom? After a horror movie marathon, it was normal to get in trouble with it. In the afterward instant, they nod their heads trying to be quieter. Suddenly, it comes to the mind of each of them, their political trajectory, their citizen side, their professional, religious side and their sexual aspect. They feel good about being imperfect devices. They were sure that qualities and defects added to their personality.

Furthermore, they lock themselves in the bathroom. By opening the shower, they let the hot water flow through the sweaty bodies due to the heat of the night before. Liquid serves as a catalyst absorbing all the bad things. That's precisely what they needed now: to forget the pain, the trauma, the disappointments, the restlessness trying to find new expectations. The current year was crucial in that. A fantastic turn in every aspect of life.

The cleaning process is initiated with the use of Plant sponges, soap, Shampoo, in addition to Water. At this time, they feel one of the best pleasures which forces you to remember the ticket on the reef and the adventures on the beach. Intuitively, their wild spirit asks for more adventures in what they stay to analyze as soon as they can. The situation favored by the time off accomplished at the work of both as a prize of dedication to public service.

For about 20 minutes, they put a little aside their goals to live a reflective moment in their respective intimacy. At the end of this activity, they come out of the toilet, wipe the wet body with the towel, wear clean clothes and shoes, wear Swiss perfume, imported makeup from Germany with very nice sunglasses and tiaras. Completely ready, they move to the cup with their purses on the strip and greet themselves happy with the reunion in thanks to the good Lord.

In cooperation, they prepare a breakfast of envy: couscous in chicken sauce, vegetables, fruit, coffee-cream and crackers. In equal parts, food is divided. They alternate moments of silence with brief exchanges of words because they were polite. Finished breakfast, there is no escape beyond what they intended.

"What do you suggest, Belinha? I'm bored!

"I have a good idea. Remember that person we met at the literary festival?

"I remember. He was a writer and his name was Divine.

"I have his number. How about we get in touch? I'd like to know where he lives.

"Me too. Great idea. Do it. I'll love it.

"All right!

Belinha opened her purse, took her phone and started dialing. In a few moments, someone answers the line and the conversation starts.

"Hello.

"Hi, Divine. All right?

"All right, Belinha. How's it going?

"We're doing fine. Look, is that invitation still on? My sister and I would like to have a special show tonight.

"Of course, I do. You won't regret it. Here we have saws, abundant nature, fresh air beyond great company. I'm available today, too.

"How wonderful. Well, wait for us at the entrance of the village. In the most 30 minutes we're almost there.

"It's ok. See you later!

"See you later!

The call ends. With a smirk stamped, Belinha returns to communicate with her sister.

"He said yes. Shall we?

"Come on. What are we waiting for?

Both parade from the cup to the exit of the house, closing the door behind them with a key. Then they move to the garage. They drive the official family car, leaving their problems behind waiting for new surprises and emotions on the most important land in the world. Through the city, with a loud sound on, kept their little hope for themselves. It was worth everything at that moment until I thought of the chance to be happy forever.

With a short time, they take the right side of highway BR 232. So, it starts the course of the course to achievement and happiness. With moderate speed, they're able to enjoy the mountain landscape on the shores of the track. Although it was a known environment, every passage there was more than a novelty. It was a rediscovered self.

Passing through places, farms, villages, blue clouds, ashes and roses, dry air and hot temperature go. In the programmed time, they're coming to the most bucolic of the entrance of the Brazilian inland. Mimoso of the colonels, the psychic, the

Immaculate Conception and people with high intellectual capacity.

When they stopped by the entrance of the district, they were expecting your dear friend with the same smile as always. A good sign for those who were looking for adventures. Getting out of the car, they go to meet the noble colleague who receives them with a hug becoming triple. This instant doesn't seem to end. They're already repeated, they start to change first impressions.

"How are you, Divine? Asked Belinha.

"Good, how are you? Corresponded the psychic.

"Great! (Belinha).

"Better than ever, complemented Amelinha.

"I have a great idea. How about we go up the Ororubá mountain? It was there exactly eight years ago that my trajectory in literature began.

"What a beauty! It will be an honor! (Amelinha).

"For me too! I love nature. (Belinha).

"So, let's go now. (Aldivan).

Signing to follow, the mysterious friend of the two sisters advanced on the streets downtown. Down to the right, entering a private place and walking about a hundred meters puts them in the bottom of the saw. They make a quick stop, so they can rest and hydrate. What was it like to climb the mountain after all these adventures? The feeling was peace, collecting, doubt and hesitation. It was like it was the first time with all the challenges taxed by fate. Suddenly, friends face the great writer with a smile.

"How did it all start? What does that mean to you? (Belinha).

"In 2009, my life revolved in monotony. What kept me alive was the will to externalize what I felt in the world. That's when I heard of this mountain and the powers of his wonderful cave. No way out, I decided to take a chance on behalf of my dream. I packed my bag, climbed the mountain, performed three challenges which I was accredited entered the grotto of despair, the most deadly, dangerous grotto in the world. Inside it, I've outdone great challenges by ending to get to the chamber. It was at that moment of ecstasy that the miracle happened, I became the psychic, an omniscient being through his visions. So far, there's been 20 more adventures and I won't stop so soon. Thanks to readers, gradually, I am achieving my goal to conquer the world.

"Exciting. I'm a fan of yours. (Amelinha).

"Touching. I know how you must feel about performing this task again. (Belinha).

"Excellent. I feel a mixture of good things including success, faith, claw, and optimism. That gives me good energy, said the psychic.

"Good. What advice do you give us?

"Let's keep our focus. Are you ready to find out better for yourselves? (the master).

"Yes. They agreed to both.

"Then follow me.

The trio has resumed the enterprise. The sun warms, the wind blows a little stronger, the birds fly away and sing, the stones and the thorns seem to move, the ground shakes and the mountain voices begin to act. This is the environment presents on the climb of the saw.

With a lot of experience, the man in the cave helps women all the time. Acting like this, he put in practical virtues important as solidarity and cooperation. In return, they lent him a human heat and unequally dedication. We could say it was that insurmountable, unstoppable, competent trio.

Little by little, they go up step by step the steps of happiness. Despite the considerable achievement, they remain tireless in their quest. In a sequel, they slow the pace of the walk a little, but keeping it steady. As the saying goes, slowly goes far away. This certainty accompanies them all the time creating a spiritual spectrum of patients, caution, tolerance and overcome. With these elements, they had faith to overcome any adversity.

The next point, the sacred stone, concludes a third of the course. There's a brief break, and they enjoy it to pray, to thank, to reflect and plan the next steps. In the right measure, they were looking to satisfy their hopes, their fears, their pain, torture, and sorrows. For having faith, an indelible peace fills their hearts.

With the reboot of the journey, the uncertainty, the doubts, and the strength of the unexpected returns to act. Although it might frighten them, they carried the safety of being in the presence of God and the little sprout of the inland. Nothing or anyone could harm them simply because God wouldn't allow it. They realized this protection at every difficult moment of life where others simply abandoned them. God is effectively our only true friend.

Further, they're half the way. The climb remains carried out with more dedication and tune. Contrary to what usually happens with ordinary climbers, rhythm helps motivation, will, and delivery. Although they weren't athletes, it was remarkable of their performance for being healthy and committed young.

After completing three quarters of the route, expectation comes to unbearable levels. How long would they have to wait? At this instant of pressure, the best thing to do was to try to control the momentum of curiosity. All careful was now due to the acting of the opposing forces.

With a little more time, they finally finish the route. The sun shines brighter, the light of God lights them up and coming out of a trail, the guardian, and his son Renato. Everything seemed to be completely reborn in the heart of those lovely little ones. They deserved that grace for having worked so hard. The next step of the psychic is to run into a tight hug with his benefactors. His colleagues follow him and make the quintuple hug.

" Good to see you, son of God! I haven't seen

you in a long time! My maternal instinct warned me of your approach, said the ancestral lady.

"I'm glad! It's like I remember my first adventure. There were so many emotions. The mountain, the challenges, the cave, and the time travel have marked my story. Coming back here brings me good reminiscences. Now, I bring with me two friendly warriors. They needed this meeting with the sacred one.

"What are your names, ladies? Asked the guardian of Mountain.

"My name is Belinha, and I'm an auditor.

"My name is Amelinha, and I'm a teacher. We live in Arcoverde.

"Welcome, ladies. (Guardian of Mountain.).

"We're grateful! Said in concomitant the two visitors with tears running through their eyes.

"I love new friendships, too. Being next to my master again gives me a special pleasure from those unspeakable. The only people who know how to understand that is the two of us. Isn't that right, partner? (Renato).

"You never change, Renato! Your words are priceless. With all my madness, finding him was one of the good things of my destiny.

THE MANIC CLOWN - 17

My friend and my brother answered the psychic without calculating the words. They came out naturally for the true feeling that nourished for him.

"We're corresponded in the same measure. That's why our story is a success, said the young man.

"How nice to be in this story. I had no idea how special the mountain was in its trajectory, dear writer, said Amelinha.

"He's really admirable, sister. Besides, your friends are very nice. We're living the real fiction and that's the most wonderful thing there is. (Belinha).

"We appreciate the compliment. However, you must be tired of the effort employed on the climbing. How about we go home? We always have something to offer. (Madame).

"We've taken the opportunity to catch up on our conversations. I miss Renato so much.

"I think it's great. As for the ladies, what do you say?

"I'll love it. (Belinha).

"We will!

"Then let's go! Has completed the master.

The quintet begins to walk in the order given by that fantastic figure. Immediately, a cold blow through the fatigued skeletons of the class. Who was that woman, actually, and what powers did she have? Despite so many moments together, the mystery remained locked as a door to seven keys. They'd probably never know because it was part of the mountain secret. Simultaneously, their hearts remained in the mist. They were exhausted from donating love and not receiving, forgiving and disappointing again. Anyway, either they got used to the reality of life or they'd suffer a lot. They needed some advice, therefore.

Step by step, they're going to get over the obstacles. Instantly, they hear a disturbing scream. With one look, the boss calms them down. That was the sense of the hierarchy, while the strongest and most experienced protected, the servants were returning with dedication, worship, and friendship. It was a two-way street.

Sadly, they'll manage the walk with great and gentleness. What the hell idea had gone through Belinha's head? They were in the middle of the bush busted by nasty animals that could hurt them. Other than that, there were thorns and

THE MANIC CLOWN - 19

pointed stones on their feet. As every situation has its point of view, being there was the only chance to understand yourself and your desires, something deficit in the lives of visitors. Soon, it was worth the adventure.

Next halfway there, they'll make a stop. Right near there, there was an orchard. They're headed for heaven. In allusion to the Bible tale, they felt completely free and integrated to nature. Like kids, they play climbing trees, they take the fruits, they come down and eat them. Then they meditate. They learned as soon as life is made by moments. Whether they're sad or happy, it's good to enjoy them while we're alive.

In the afterward instant, they take a refreshing bath in the lake attached. This fact provokes good memories of once, of the most remarkable experiences in their lives. How nice it was to be a child! How hard it was to grow up and face adult life. Live with the false, the lie and the false morality of people.

Moving on, they're approaching destiny. Down the right on the trail, you can already see the simple hovel. That was the sanctuary of the most wonderful, mysterious people on the mountain. They were wonderful, what proves that a person's value is not in what it possesses. The nobility of the soul is in character, in charity and counseling attitudes. So, the saying goes: a friend in the square is better than money deposited in a bank.

A few steps forward, they stop in front of the entrance of the cabin. Will they get answers to your inner inquiries? Only time could answer this and other questions. The important thing about this was that they were there for whatever comes and goes.

Taking the hostess's role, the guardian opens the door, giving everyone else access to the inside of the house. They enter the empty cubicle, observing everything widely. They are impressed with the delicacy of the place represented by the ornamentation, the objects, the furniture, and the climate of mystery. Contradictory, there were more riches and cultural diversity than in many palaces. So, we can feel happy and complete even in humble environments.

One by one, you'll settle in at the available locations, except Renato's going to the kitchen to prepare lunch. The initial climate of shyness is broken.

"I'd like to know you better, girls.

THE MANIC CLOWN - 21

"We're two girls from Arcoverde City. We are happy professionally, but losers in love. Ever since I was betrayed by my old partner, I've been frustrated, Confessed Belinha.

"That's when we decided to get back at men. We made a pact to lure them and use them as an object. We'll never suffer again, said Amelinha.

"I give them all my support. I met them in the crowd and now their opportunity has come to visit here. (son of God)

"Interesting. This is a natural reaction to the suffering of disappointments. However, it's not the best way to be followed. Judging an entire species by a person's attitude is a clear mistake. Each has its individuality. This sacred and shameless face of yours can generate more conflict and pleasure. It's up to you to find the right point of this story. What I can do is support as your friend did and become an accessory to this story analyzed the sacred spirit of the mountain.

"I'll allow it. I want to find myself in this shrine. (Amelinha).

"I accept your friendship too. Who knew I'd be on a fantastic soap opera? The myth of the cave and mountain seem so real now. Can I make a wish? (Belinha).

"Of course, dear.

"The mountain entities can hear the requests of the humble dreamers as it has happened to me. Have faith! (the son of God).

"I'm so disbelieved. But if you say so, I'll try. I ask for a happy ending for all of us. Let each of you come true in the main fields of life.

"I grant it! Thunders a deep voice in the middle of the room.

Both whores have made a jump to the ground. Meanwhile, the others laughed and cried at the reaction of both. That fact had been more of a fate action. What a surprise. There was no one who could have predicted what was happening on top of the mountain. Since a famous Indian had died at the scene, the sensation of reality had left room for the supernatural, the mystery and the unusual.

"What the hell was that thunder? I'm shaking so far, confessed Amelinha.

"I heard what the voice said. She confirmed my wish. Am I dreaming? Asked Belinha.

"Miracles happen! In time, you'll know exactly what it means to say this, said the master.

"I believe in the mountain, and you must believe in it too. Through her miracle, I remain here convinced and safe of my decisions. If we fail once, we can start over. There's always hope for those alive- assured the shaman of the psychic showing a signal on the roof.

"A light. What does that mean? (Belinha).

"It's so beautiful and bright. (Amelinha).

"It's the light of our eternal friendship. Though she disappears physically, she will remain intact in our hearts. (Guardian

"We are all light, though in distinguished ways. Our destiny is happiness. (the psychic).

That's where Renato comes in and makes a proposition.

"It's time we went out and found some friends. Time for fun has come.

"I'm looking forward to it. (Belinha)

"What are we waiting for? It's time. (SCREAMS)

The quartet goes out in the woods. The pace of steps is fast what reveals an inner anguish of the characters. Mimoso's rural environment contributed to a spectacle of nature. What challenges would you face? Would the fierce animals be dangerous? The mountain myths could attack at any time which was quite dangerous. But courage was a quality that everyone there carried. Nothing will stop their happiness.

The time has come. On the asset team, there was a black man, Renato, and a blond. On the passive team was Divine, Belinha and Amelinha. with the team formed, the fun begins among the gray green from the country woods.

The black guy dates Divine. Renato Dates Amelinha and the blond man dates Belinha. Group sex starts at the exchange of energy between the six. They were all for one and all for one. The thirst for sex and pleasure was common to all. Changing positions, each one experiences unique sensations. They try anal sex, vaginal sex, oral sex, group sex among other sex modalities. That proves love is not a sin. It's a trade of fundamental energy for human evolution. Without guilt, they quickly exchange partner, which provides multiple orgasms. It's a mixture of ecstasy that involves the group. They spend hours having sex until they're tired.

After all is completed, they return to their initial positions. There was still a lot to discover on the mountain.

The end

www.ingramcontent.com/pod-product-compliance
Lightning Source LLC
LaVergne TN
LVHW020454080526
838202LV00055B/5445